A Christmas Carol

in Prose
Being a Ghost Story of Christmas

Charles Dickens

ROUTLEDGE & KEGAN PAUL

London

First published 1965
by The Dickens House, London
This edition first published 1972
by Routledge & Kegan Paul Ltd
Broadway House, 68-74 Carter Lane,
London EC4V 5EL

Printed in Great Britain by
Lewis Reprints Ltd.
member of Brown Knight & Truscott Group
London and Tonbridge

ISBN 0 7100 7443 3

Dedicated to
all those lovers of Charles Dickens
throughout the world

The illustrations in this book are
by Charles Wilton. We are very grateful to
The Nimrod Press, Boston, USA
for granting us permission to use them

The designer and production adviser
for this edition was Owen Griffiths

Contents

Preface

By Henry Charles Dickens OBE
Life President of the Dickens Fellowship

The story that gave my grandfather the greatest pleasure in writing was undoubtedly 'A Christmas Carol'. In a letter he wrote to his American friend, Professor Felton, in January 1844, he said: 'Over which Christmas Carol Charles Dickens wept and laughed and wept again, and excited himself in a most extraordinary manner in the composition; and thinking whereof he walked about the black streets of London, fifteen and twenty miles many a night when all the sober folks had gone to bed. . . .

The aim and thought behind it can best be expressed in my grandfather's own words in his Preface to the first edition —

I have endeavoured in this Ghostly little book, to raise the Ghost of an Idea, which shall not put my readers out of humour with themselves, with each other, with the season, or with me. May it haunt their houses pleasantly, and no one wish to lay it.

It has remained one of the most popular and frequently read of his stories, familiar to both young and old alike. People of all nations read it as Christmas comes round, often aloud. My father read it to us when we were children -- as many other fathers have done all over the world since the publication of 'Christmas Books', and he had the great pleasure and advantage of having heard his father read it himself many and many times.

He read (recited is a better word) from the authentic version adapted by his father for his readings, with all the traditional changes of mood, from the horrific to the farcical, and from the pathetic to the language of Christianity. We soon learned to be horrified with Jacob Marley — to weep for the death of Tiny Tim and revel with the Fezziwigs and the prize turkey — 'the one as big as me'.

May you all share these delights with or without your young ones. Don't jibe at 'Carol Philosophy' — many of us prefer it to kitchen-sink philosophy!

Henry C. Dickens

Foreword

By Cedric C. Dickens
President of the Dickens Fellowship

Emlyn Williams, that modern reader of Dickens, once said that Charles Dickens had been 'tried for sound'. What he meant was that in writing his stories my greatgrandfather had the sound version in his mind of the words he was using. This is why the words of Dickens lend themselves so readily to being read aloud and why so many people — actors, broadcasters, lecturers, family groups — still find so many excellent subjects in his books for reading aloud. Charles Dickens himself did. Audiences, both public and private, really enjoy hearing his stories read.

Although the novelist in his preface to 'A Christmas Carol' apologised for not attempting 'great elaboration of detail in the working out of character', what more can a reader wish for than the clear description of the character of Ebenezer Scrooge '. . . a squeezing, wrenching, grasping, scraping, clutching, covetous old sinner! Hard and sharp as flint, from which no steel had ever struck out generous fire; secret and self-contained, and solitary as an oyster. The cold within him froze his old features, nipped his pointed nose, shrivelled his cheek, stiffened his gait; made his eyes red, his thin lips blue; and spoke out shrewdly in his grating voice. . . .'

Or of his nephew — 'He had so heated himself with rapid walking in the fog and frost . . . that he was all in a glow; his face was ruddy and handsome; his eyes sparkled, and his breath smoked again!' Examples could be given of a dozen or more other characters even in this short story.

With such exciting and choice words at his disposal, the reader can play upon the imaginations of an audience as a musician plays upon a sensitive instrument. A slight inflection of the voice, an appropriate expression of the face, the character is brought to life, and the fortunate reader will be credited by the reactions of the audience, with powers he hardly knew he possessed. 'How *do* you make yourself look like these characters!' The answer is that it is there, in Dickens, and the reader has only to grasp the opportunity.

Reading Dickens aloud is nevertheless a challenge — a challenge to re-create the original thoughts of the writer and to re-capture the thrill he must have experienced as the characters and scenes unfolded themselves for the first time on the blank paper before him. But to read *The Carol* aloud is a special experience. The best Dickens subject of all for such purpose; for, after all, did not Dickens choose this story first and foremost and keep it in his repertoire until the very last reading? He knew only too well its great value. John Greaves, that epic Pickwickian and Hon. Secretary of the Dickens Fellowship, ought to know. He has read Dickens all over the world to thousands of people and is remembered with affection.

'To read it aloud', he says, 'is a wonderful experience, but at the same time, a great ordeal, for in the interpretation of such a story, one cannot remain entirely outside. To give it conscientiously, one cannot help experiencing the emotions and reactions of the characters involved, and all the time feeling their impact upon the central character, Scrooge. To give a reading of *The Carol* is to live a lifetime in one hour — as Scrooge so aptly remarks at the end — *The Spirits have done it all in one night!*

Scrooge in the beginning to any reader worth his salt, is theatrical 'jam' — a ready made character part, with comedy and melodrama, mixed by the hand of an expert — one can hardly go wrong. But Scrooge at the end is a far more difficult proposition. To keep up the bubbling, hysterical, enthusiasm of the old man, now quite childish but sincere, playing it all at a high level and on one level as it were, is extremely difficult and very exhausting. Even so, it can only be convincing if the proper degrees of gradual remorse have been maintained during the transitional period. Every point in the three dreams must make its mark, and must be apparent, and what is more, Scrooge must not go back one step once an effect is shown. He must go on and on, until at last he is ready for the final climax of hysterical joy, and gathering his bedcurtains in his arms, declares — 'They are not torn down, rings and all. They are here — I am here — the shadows of the things that would have been may be dispelled. They will be. I know they will!' Then the end can be convincing, but what havoc it can play with the reader's feelings and with the feelings of his audience if he has presented the whole thing correctly—That is the challenge of *The Carol* and one always found most stimulating and rewarding.

Always try to imagine reading it to a family round the fireside. That is the atmosphere one needs —the shadowy light of candles and flickering firelight; the warmth and friendliness of a

Marley's Ghost

ARLEY was dead: to begin with. There is no doubt whatever about that. The register of his burial was signed by the clergyman, the clerk, the undertaker, and the chief mourner. Scrooge signed it: and Scrooge's name was good upon 'Change, for anything he chose to put his hand to. Old Marley was as dead as a door-nail.

Scrooge knew he was dead? Of course he did. How could it be otherwise? Scrooge and he were partners for I don't know how many years. Scrooge was his sole executor, his sole administrator, his sole assign, his sole residuary legatee, his sole friend, and sole mourner. And even Scrooge was not so dreadfully cut up by the sad event, but he was an excellent man of business on the very day of the funeral, and solemnised it with an undoubted bargain.

Scrooge never painted out Old Marley's name. There it stood, years afterwards, above the warehouse door:

Scrooge and Marley. Sometimes people new to the business called Scrooge Scrooge, and sometimes Marley, but he answered to both names. It was all the same to him.

Oh! But he was a tight-fisted hand at the grindstone, Scrooge, a squeezing, wrenching, grasping, scraping, clutching, covetous old sinner! Hard and sharp as flint, from which no steel had ever struck out generous fire; secret, and self-contained, and solitary as an oyster. The cold within him froze his old features, nipped his pointed nose, shrivelled his cheek, stiffened his gait; made his eyes red, his thin lips blue; and spoke out shrewdly in his grating voice.

External heat and cold had little influence on him. No warmth could warm, nor wintry weather chill him. No wind that blew was bitterer than he, no falling snow was more intent upon its purpose, no pelting rain less open to entreaty. The heaviest rain, and snow, and hail, and sleet, could boast of the advantage over him in only one respect. They often 'came down' handsomely, and Scrooge never did.

Once upon a time — of all the good days in the year, on Christmas Eve — old Scrooge sat busy in his counting-house. It was cold, bleak, biting weather: foggy withal. The city clocks had only just gone three, but it was quite dark already: it had not been light all day: and candles were flaring in the windows of the neighbouring offices, like ruddy smears upon the palpable brown air. The fog came pouring in at every chink and keyhole, and was so

dense without, that although the court was of the narrow-
est, the houses opposite were mere phantoms. To see the
dingy cloud come drooping down, obscuring everything,
one might have thought that Nature lived hard by and was
brewing on a large scale.

The door of Scrooge's counting-house was open that
he might keep his eye upon his clerk, who in a dismal little
cell beyond, a sort of tank, was copying letters. Scrooge
had a very small fire, but the clerk's fire was so very much
smaller that it looked like one coal. But he couldn't re-
plenish it, for Scrooge kept the coal-box in his own room;
and so surely as the clerk came in with the shovel, the
master predicted that it would be necessary for them to
part. Wherefore the clerk put on his white comforter, and
tried to warm himself at the candle; in which effort, not
being a man of a strong imagination, he failed.

'A merry Christmas, uncle! God save you!' cried a
cheerful voice. It was the voice of Scrooge's nephew, who
came upon him so quickly that this was the first intimation
he had of his approach.

'Bah!' said Scrooge, 'Humbug!'

'Christmas a humbug, uncle! You don't mean that, I
am sure.'

'I do. Merry Christmas! Out upon merry Christmas:
What's Christmas time to you but a time for paying bills
without money; a time for finding yourself a year older,
and not an hour richer; a time for balancing your books

and having every item in 'em through a round dozen of months presented dead against you? If I could work my will, every idiot who goes about with "Merry Christmas" on his lips, should be boiled with his own pudding, and buried with a stake of holly through his heart. He should!'

'Uncle!'

'Nephew! Keep Christmas in your own way, and let me keep it in mine.'

'Keep it! But you don't keep it.'

'Let me leave it alone, then. Much good may it do you! Much good it has ever done you!'

'There are many things from which I might have derived good, by which I have not profited, I dare say: Christmas among the rest. But I am sure I have always thought of Christmas time, when it has come round — apart from the veneration due to its sacred name and origin, if anything belonging to it can be apart from that — as a good time: a kind, forgiving, charitable, pleasant time: the only time I know of, in the long calendar of the year, when men and women seem by one consent to open their shut-up hearts freely, and to think of people below them as if they really were fellow-passengers to the grave, and not another race of creatures bound on other journeys. And therefore, uncle, though it has never put a scrap of gold or silver in my pocket, I believe that it *has* done me good, and *will* do me good; and I say, God bless it!'

The clerk in the tank involuntarily applauded; becoming immediately sensible of the impropriety, he poked the fire, and extinguished the last frail spark for ever.

'Let me hear another sound from *you*,' said Scrooge, 'and you'll keep your Christmas by losing your situation.' And to his nephew 'You're quite a powerful speaker, sir. I wonder you don't go into Parliament.'

'Don't be angry, uncle. Come! Dine with us to-morrow.'

Scrooge said that he would see him — yes, indeed he did. He went the whole length of the expression, and said that he would see him in that extremity first.

'But why? Why?'

'Why did you get married?'

'Because I fell in love.'

'Because you fell in love! Good afternoon!'

'I am sorry, with all my heart, to find you so resolute. But I have made the trial in homage to Christmas, and I'll keep my Christmas humour to the last. So A Merry Christmas, uncle!'

'Good afternoon!'

'And A Happy New Year!'

'Good afternoon!'

His nephew left the room without an angry word, notwithstanding. He stopped at the outer door to bestow the greetings of the season on the clerk, who, cold as he was, was warmer than Scrooge; for he returned them cordially.

'There's another fellow,' muttered Scrooge, who overheard him: 'my clerk, with fifteen shillings a week, and a

wife and family, talking about a merry Christmas. I'll retire to Bedlam.'

The clerk, in letting Scrooge's nephew out, had let two
other people in. They were portly gentlemen, pleasant to
behold, and now stood, with their hats off, in Scrooge's
office. They had books and papers in their hands, and
bowed to him.

'Scrooge and Marley's, I believe,' said one of the gentlemen, referring to his list. 'Have I the pleasure of address-
ing Mr Scrooge, or Mr Marley?'

'Mr Marley has been dead these seven years,' Scrooge
replied. 'He died seven years ago, this very night.'

'At this festive season of the year, Mr Scrooge,' said
the gentleman, taking up a pen, 'it is more than usually
desirable that we should make some slight provision for the
Poor and destitute, who suffer greatly at the present time.
Many thousands are in want of common necessaries;
hundreds of thousands are in want of common comforts, sir.'

'Are there no prisons?'

'Plenty of prisons.'

'And the Union workhouses?' demanded Scrooge. 'Are
they still in operation?'

'They are. But under the impression that they scarcely
furnish Christian cheer of mind or body to the multitude,
a few of us are endeavouring to raise a fund to buy the
Poor some meat and drink, and means of warmth. We
choose this time, because it is a time, of all others, when

Want is keenly felt, and Abundance rejoices. What shall I put you down for?'

'Nothing!'

'You wish to be anonymous?'

'I wish to be left alone. Since you ask me what I wish, gentlemen, that is my answer. I don't make merry myself at Christmas and I can't afford to make idle people merry. I help to support the prisons and workhouses: they cost enough: and those who are badly off must go there.'

'Many can't go there; and many would rather die.'

'If they would rather die, they had better do it, and decrease the surplus population. Good afternoon, gentlemen!'

Seeing clearly that it would be useless to pursue their point, the gentlemen withdrew.

Foggier yet, and colder! Piercing, searching, biting cold. The owner of one scant young nose, gnawed and mumbled by the hungry cold as bones are gnawed by dogs, stooped down at Scrooge's keyhole to regale him with a Christmas carol: but at the first sound of

'God bless you, merry gentleman!
May nothing you dismay!'

Scrooge seized the ruler with such energy of action that the singer fled in terror, leaving the keyhole to the fog and even more congenial frost.

At length the hour of shutting up the counting-house arrived. With an ill-will Scrooge dismounted from his stool, and tacitly admitted the fact to the expectant clerk in the Tank, who instantly snuffed his candle out, and put on his hat.

'You'll want all day to-morrow, I suppose?'

'If quite convenient, Sir.'

'It's not convenient, and it's not fair. If I was to stop half-a-crown for it, you'd think yourself ill used, I'll be bound?'

The clerk smiled faintly.

'And yet, you don't think *me* ill-used, when I pay a day's wages for no work.'

The clerk observed that it was only once a year.

'A poor excuse for picking a man's pocket every twenty-fifth of December! But I suppose you must have the whole day. Be here all the earlier next morning!'

The clerk promised that he would; and Scrooge walked out with a growl. The office was closed in a twinkling, and the clerk, with the long ends of his white comforter dangling below his waist (for he boasted no great-coat), went down a slide on Cornhill, at the end of a lane of boys, twenty times, in honour of its being Christmas-eve, and then ran home to Camden Town as hard as he could pelt, to play at blindman's-buff.

Scrooge took his melancholy dinner in his usual melancholy tavern; and having read all the newspapers, and beguiled the rest of the evening with his banker's-book, went home to bed. He lived in chambers which had once belonged to his deceased partner. They were a gloomy suite of rooms, in a lowering pile of building up a yard, where it had so little business to be, that one could scarcely help fancying it must have run there when it was a young house, playing at hide-and-seek with other houses, and have forgotten the way out again.

Now, it is a fact, that there was nothing at all particular about the knocker on the door, except that it was very large. It is also a fact, that Scrooge had seen it night and morning during his whole residence in that place; also that Scrooge had as little of what is called fancy about him as any man in the City of London, yet Scrooge, having his key in the lock of the door, saw in the knocker, without its undergoing any intermediate process of change: not a knocker, but Marley's face.

Marley's face, with a dismal light about it, like a bad lobster in a dark cellar. It was not angry or ferocious, but looked at Scrooge as Marley used to look: with ghostly spectacles turned up upon its ghostly forehead. As Scrooge looked fixedly at this phenomenon, it was a knocker again.

To say that he was not startled, or that his blood was not conscious of a terrible sensation to which it had been a stranger from infancy, would be untrue. But he put his hand upon the key he had relinquished, turned it sturdily, walked in, and lighted his candle.

He *did* pause, with a moment's irresolution, before he shut the door; and he *did* look cautiously behind it first, as if he half-expected to be terrified with the sight of Marley's pigtail sticking out into the hall. But there was nothing on the back of the door, except the screws and nuts that held the knocker on, so he said 'Pooh, pooh!' and closed it with a bang.

The sound resounded through the house like thunder. Every room above, and every cask in the wine-merchant's cellars below, appeared to have a separate peal of echoes of its own. Scrooge was not a man to be frightened by echoes. He fastened the door, and walked across the hall, and up the stairs, slowly too: trimming his candle as he went, for it was very dark.

Up Scrooge went, not caring a button for that: darkness is cheap, and Scrooge liked it. But before he shut his heavy door, he walked through his rooms to see that all was right. He had just enough recollection of the face to desire to do that.

Sitting-room, bed-room, lumber-room. All as they should be. Nobody under the table, nobody under the sofa; a small fire in the grate; spoon and basin ready; and the little saucepan of gruel (Scrooge had a cold in his head) upon the hob. Nobody under the bed; nobody in the closet; nobody in his dressing-gown, which was hanging up in a suspicious attitude against the wall. Quite satisfied, he closed his door, and locked himself in; double-locked himself in, which was not his custom. Thus secured against surprise, he took off his cravat; put on his dressing-gown and slippers, and his night-cap; and sat down before the fire to take his gruel.

As he threw his head back in the chair, his glance happened to rest upon a bell, a disused bell, that hung in the room, and communicated for some purpose now forgotten with a chamber in the highest story of the building. It was with great astonishment, and with a strange, inexplicable dread, that as he looked, he saw this bell begin to swing. Soon it rang out loudly, and so did every bell in the house.

The bells ceased as they had begun, together. They were succeeded by a clanking noise, deep down below; as if some person were dragging a heavy chain over the casks in the wine-merchant's cellar. The cellar-door flew open with a booming sound, and then he heard the noise much louder, on the floors below; then coming up the stairs; then coming straight towards his door.

Then, without a pause, it came on through the heavy door, and passed into the room before his eyes. Upon its coming in, the dying flame leaped up, as though it cried 'I know him! Marley's Ghost!' and fell again.

The same face: the very same. Marley in his pig-tail, usual waistcoat, tights, and boots. The chain he drew was clasped about his middle. It was long, and wound about him like a tail; and it was made (for Scrooge observed it closely) of cashboxes, keys, padlocks, ledgers, deeds, and heavy purses wrought in steel. His body was transparent: so that Scrooge, observing him, and looking through his waistcoat, could see the two buttons on his coat behind.

Scrooge had often heard it said that Marley had no bowels, but he had never believed it until now.

'How now!' said Scrooge, caustic and cold as ever. 'What do you want with me?'

'Much!' — Marley's voice, no doubt about it.

'Who are you?'

'Ask me who I *was*.'

'Who *were* you then? You're particular — for a shade.'

'In life I was your partner, Jacob Marley.'

'Can you — can you sit down?'

'I can.'

'Do it then.'

Scrooge asked the question, because he didn't know whether a ghost so transparent might find himself in a condition to take a chair; and felt that in the event of its being impossible, it might involve the necessity of an embarrassing explanation.

'You don't believe in me.'

'I don't.'

'What evidence would you have of my reality beyond that of your senses? Why do you doubt your senses?'

'Because a little thing affects them. A slight disorder of the stomach makes them cheats. You may be an undigested bit of beef, a blot of mustard, a crumb of cheese, a fragment of an underdone potato. There's more of gravy than of grave about you, whatever you are!'

Scrooge was not much in the habit of cracking jokes, nor did he feel, in his heart, by any means waggish, then. The truth is, that he tried to be smart, as a means of distracting his own attention, and keeping down his terror. But how much greater was his horror when, taking off the bandage round its head, as if it were too warm to wear indoors, the phantom's lower jaw dropped down upon its breast!

'Mercy! Dreadful apparition, why do you trouble me? Why do spirits walk the earth, and why do they come to me?'

'It is required of every man, that the spirit within him should walk abroad among his fellow-men, and travel far and wide; and if that spirit goes not forth in life, it is condemned to do so after death. It is doomed to wander through the world — oh, woe is me! — and witness what it cannot share, but might have shared on earth, and turned to happiness!'

'You are fettered, tell me why?'

'I wear the chain I forged in life,' replied the Ghost. 'I made it link by link, and yard by yard; I girded it on of my own free will, and of my own free will I wore it. Is its pattern strange to *you*? Or would you know the weight and length of the strong coil you bear yourself? It was full as heavy and as long as this, seven Christmas Eves ago. You have laboured on it, since. It is a ponderous chain!'

Scrooge glanced about him on the floor, in the expectation of finding himself surrounded by some fifty or sixty fathoms of iron cable; but he could see nothing.

'Jacob. Old Jacob Marley, tell me more. Speak comfort to me, Jacob.'

'I have none to give,' the Ghost replied. 'It comes from other regions, Ebenezer Scrooge, and is conveyed by other ministers, to other kinds of men. Nor can I tell you what I would. A very little more, is all that is permitted to me. I cannot rest, I cannot stay, I cannot linger anywhere. My spirit never walked beyond our counting-house — mark me! — in life my spirit never roved beyond the narrow limits of our money-changing hole; and weary journeys lie before me!'

'You might have got over a great quantity of ground in seven years!'

'Oh! captive, bound, and double-ironed, not to know that no space of regret can make amends for one life's opportunities misused! Yet such was I! Oh! such was I! Hear me! My time is nearly gone.'

'I will. But don't be hard upon me! Don't be flowery, Jacob!'

'I am here to-night to warn you that you have yet a chance and hope of escaping my fate. A chance and hope of my procuring, Ebenezer.'

'You were always a good friend to me. Thank'ee!'

'You will be haunted by Three Spirits.'

'Is that the chance and hope you mentioned, Jacob?'

'It is.'

'I — I think I'd rather not.'

'Without their visits you cannot hope to shun the path I tread. Expect the first to-morrow, when the bell tolls One. Expect the second on the next night at the same hour. The third upon the next night when the last stroke of Twelve has ceased to vibrate. Look to see me no more; and look that, for your own sake, you remember what has passed between us!'

When it had said these words, the spectre took its wrapper from the table and bound it round its head, as before. Scrooge knew this, by the smart sound its teeth made, when the jaws were brought together by the bandage.

The apparition walked backward from him; and at every step it took, the window raised itself a little, so that when the spectre reached it, it was wide open. It beckoned Scrooge to approach, which he did.

The spectre floated out through the self-opened window into the bleak, dark night.

Scrooge closed the window, and examined the door by which the Ghost had entered. It was double-locked, as he had locked it with his own hands, and the bolts were undisturbed. He tried to say 'Humbug!' but stopped at the first syllable. And being, from the emotion he had undergone, or the fatigues of the day, or the dull conversation of the Ghost, or the lateness of the hour, much in need of repose; went straight to bed, without undressing, and fell asleep on the instant.

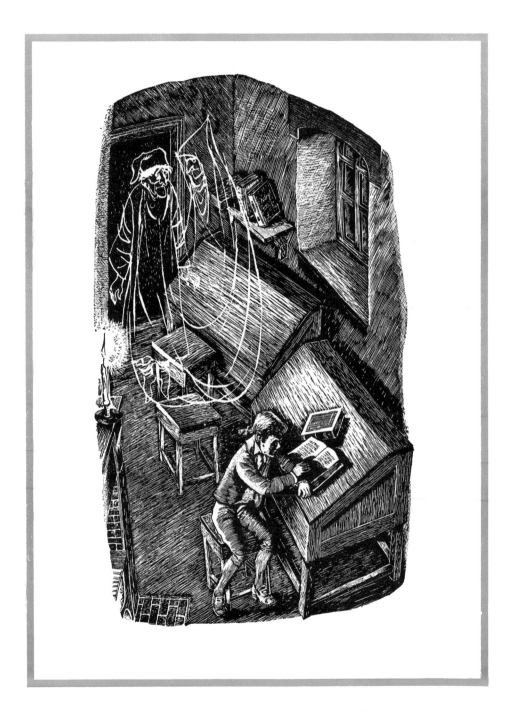

Stave Two
The First of
the Three Spirits

WHEN Scrooge awoke, it was so dark that, looking out of bed, he could scarcely distinguish the transparent window from the opaque walls of his chamber. Suddenly the church clock tolled a deep, dull, hollow, melancholy ONE. Light flashed up in the room upon the instant, the curtains of his bed were drawn aside, and Scrooge, starting up into a half-recumbent attitude, found himself face to face with the unearthly visitor who drew them.

It was a strange figure — like a child: yet not so like a child as like an old man viewed through some supernatural medium, which gave him the appearance of having receded from the view and being diminished to a child's proportions. Its hair, which hung about its neck and down its back, was white as if with age; and yet the face had not a wrinkle in it, and the tenderest bloom was on the skin. It held a branch of fresh green holly in its hand; and, in

singular contradiction of that wintry emblem, had its
dress trimmed with summer flowers. But the strangest thing
about it was, that from the crown of its head there sprung
a bright clear jet of light, by which all this was visible; and
which was doubtless the occasion of its using, in its duller
moments, a great extinguisher for a cap, which it now held
under its arm.

'Are you the Spirit, sir, whose coming was foretold to
me?'

'I am!'

'Who, and what are you?'

'I am the Ghost of Christmas Past.'

'Long past?' inquired Scrooge: observant of its dwarf-
ish stature.

'No. Your past. The things that you will see with me
are shadows of the things that have been. They will have
no consciousness of us. Rise and walk with me.'

It would have been in vain for Scrooge to plead that
the weather and the hour were not adapted to pedestrian
purposes; that bed was warm, and the thermometer a long
way below freezing; that he was clad but lightly in his slippers, dressing-gown, and nightcap; and that he had a cold
upon him at that time. The grasp, though gentle as a
woman's hand, was not to be resisted. He arose: but finding that the Spirit made towards the window, clasped its
robe in supplication.

'I am a mortal, and liable to fall.'

'Bear but a touch of my hand *there*,' said the Spirit, laying it upon his heart, 'and you shall be upheld in more than this!'

As the words were spoken, they passed through the wall, and stood on an open country road, with snow upon the ground.

'Good Heaven! I was bred in this place. I was a boy here!'

'Your lip is trembling,' said the Ghost. 'And what is that upon your cheek?'

Scrooge muttered, with an unusual catching in his voice, that it was a pimple.

'You recollect the way?' inquired the Spirit.

'Remember it! I could walk it blindfold.'

'Strange to have forgotten it for so many years! Let us go on.'

They walked along the road; Scrooge recognising every gate, and post, and tree; until a little market-town appeared in the distance, with its bridge, its church, and winding river and school.

'The school is not quite deserted,' said the Ghost. 'A solitary child, neglected by his friends, is left there still.'

Scrooge said he knew it. And he sobbed.

At one of these desks a lonely boy was reading near a feeble fire; and Scrooge sat down upon a form, and wept to see his poor forgotten self as he had used to be.

'Poor boy! I wish, but it's too late now.'

'What is the matter?' asked the Spirit.

'Nothing,' said Scrooge. 'Nothing. There was a boy singing a Christmas Carol at my door last night. I should like to have given him something: that's all.'

The Ghost smiled thoughtfully.

Although they had but that moment left the school behind them, they were now in the busy thoroughfares of a city.

The Ghost stopped at a certain warehouse door, and asked Scrooge if he knew it.

'Know it! I was apprenticed here!'

They went in. At sight of an old gentleman in a Welch wig, sitting behind such a high desk, that if he had been two inches taller he must have knocked his head against the ceiling, Scrooge cried in great excitement:

'Why, it's old Fezziwig! Bless his heart; it's Fezziwig alive again!'

Old Fezziwig laid down his pen, and looked up at the clock, which pointed to the hour of seven. He rubbed his hands; adjusted his capacious waistcoat; laughed all over himself, from his shoes to his organ of benevolence; and called out in a comfortable, oily, rich, fat, jovial voice:

'Yo ho, there! Ebenezer! Dick!'

Scrooge's former self came briskly in, accompanied by his fellow-'prentice.

'Dick Wilkins, to be sure! Bless me, yes. There he is.

He was very much attached to me, was Dick. Poor Dick! Dear, dear!'

'Yo ho, my boys!' said Fezziwig. 'No more work to-night. Christmas Eve, Dick. Christmas, Ebenezer! Let's have the shutters up before a man can say, Jack Robinson!'

You wouldn't believe how those two fellows went at it! They charged into the street with the shutters — one, two, three — had 'em up in their places — four, five, six — barred 'em and pinned 'em — seven, eight, nine — and came back before you could have got to twelve, panting like race-horses.

'Hilli ho!' cried old Fezziwig, skipping down from the high desk, with wonderful agility. 'Clear away, my lads, and let's have lots of room here! Hilli-ho, Dick! Chirrup, Ebenezer!'

Clear away! There was nothing they wouldn't have cleared away, or couldn't have cleared away, with old Fezziwig looking on. It was done in a minute. Every movable was packed off, as if it were dismissed from public life for evermore; the floor was swept and watered, the lamps were trimmed, fuel was heaped upon the fire; and the warehouse was as snug, and warm, and dry, and bright a ball-room, as you would desire to see upon a winter's night.

In came a fiddler with a music book, and went up to the lofty desk, and made an orchestra of it, and tuned like fifty stomach-aches. In came Mrs Fezziwigg, one vast

substantial smile. In came three Miss Fezziwigs, beaming
and lovable. In came the six young followers whose hearts
they broke. In came all the young men and women em-
ployed in the business. In came the housemaid, with her
cousin, the baker. In came the cook, with her brother's
particular friend, the milkman. In they all came, one after
another; some shyly, some boldly, some gracefully, some
awkwardly, some pushing, some pulling; in they all came,
anyhow and everyhow. Away they all went twenty couple
at once, hands half round and back again the other way;
down the middle and up again; round and round in various stages of affectionate grouping; old top couple always
turning up in the wrong place; new top couple starting off
again, as soon as they got there; all top couples at last, and
not a bottom one to help them. When this result was
brought about, old Fezziwig, clapping his hands to stop
the dance, cried out, 'Well done!' and the fiddler plunged
his hot face into a pot of porter, especially provided for that
purpose.

There were more dances, and there were forfeits, and
more dances, and there was cake, and there was negus, and
there was a great piece of Cold Roast, and there was a
great piece of Cold Boiled, and there were mince-pies, and
plenty of beer. But the great effect of the evening came after
the Roast and Boiled, when the fiddler struck up 'Sir
Roger de Coverley'. Then old Fezziwig stood out to dance
with Mrs Fezziwig. Top couple too; with a good stiff piece

of work cut out for them; three or four and twenty pair of partners; people who were not to be trifled with; people who *would* dance, and had no notion of walking.

But if they had been twice as many: ah, four times: old Fezziwig would have been a match for them, and so would Mrs Fezziwig. As to *her*, she was worthy to be his partner in every sense of the term. A positive light appeared to issue from Fezziwig's calves. They shone in every part of the dance like moons. You couldn't have predicted, at any given time, what would become of 'em next. And when old Fezziwig and Mrs Fezziwig had gone all through the dance; advance and retire, hold hands with your partner; bow and curtsey; corkscrew; thread-the-needle, and back again to your place; Fezziwig 'cut' — cut so deftly, that he appeared to wink with his legs.

When the clock struck eleven, this domestic ball broke up. Mr and Mrs Fezziwig took their stations, one on either side of the door, and shaking hands with every person individually as he or she went out, wished him or her a Merry Christmas. When everybody had retired but the two 'prentices, they did the same to them; and thus the cheerful voices died away, and the lads were left to their beds; which were under a counter in the back-shop.

'A small matter,' said the Ghost, 'to make these silly folks so full of gratitude.'

'Small!' echoed Scrooge.

'Why! Is it not? He has spent but a few pounds of

your mortal money: three or four, perhaps. Is that so much
that he deserves this praise?'

'It isn't that,' said Scrooge, heated by the remark, and
speaking unconsciously like his former, not his latter, self.
'It isn't that, Spirit. He has the power to render us happy
or unhappy; to make our service light or burdensome; a
pleasure or a toil.'

He felt the Spirit's glance, and stopped.

'What is the matter?'

'Nothing particular.'

'Something, I think?'

'No. No. I should like to be able to say a word or two
to my clerk just now! That's all.'

His former self turned down the lamps as he gave utter-
ance to the wish; and Scrooge and the Ghost again stood
side by side in the open air.

'My time grows short,' observed the Spirit.

Again Scrooge saw himself. He was older now; a man
in the prime of life.

He was not alone, but sat by the side of a fair young
girl in a black dress: in whose eyes there were tears, which
sparkled in the light that shone out of the Ghost of Christmas Past.

'It matters little,' she said, softly to Scrooge's former
self. 'To you, very little. Another idol has displaced me;
and if it can cheer and comfort you in time to come, as I
would have tried to do, I have no just cause to grieve.'

'What Idol has displaced you?' he rejoined.

'A golden one.'

'Spirit! show me no more! Why do you delight to torture me?'

'One shadow more!'

They were in another scene and place: a room, not very large or handsome, but full of comfort. Near to the winter fire sat a beautiful young girl, so like the last that Scrooge believed it was the same, until he saw *her,* now a comely matron, sitting opposite her daughter. The noise in this room was perfectly tumultuous, for there were more children there than Scrooge in his agitated state of mind could count, but no one seemed to care; on the contrary, the mother and daughter laughed heartily. But now a knocking at the door was heard, and such a rush immediately ensued that the daughter was borne towards it, the centre of a flushed and boisterous group, just in time to greet the father, laden with Christmas toys and presents.

The shouts of wonder and delight with which every package was received! The terrible announcement that the baby had been taken in the act of putting a doll's frying-pan into his mouth, and was more than suspected of having swallowed a fictitious turkey, glued on a wooden platter! The immense relief of finding this a false alarm! By degrees the children were got out of the parlour and by one stair at a time, up to the top of the house; where they went to bed, and so subsided.

25

And now Scrooge looked on more attentively than ever, when the master of the house, having his daughter leaning fondly on him, sat down with her and her mother at his own fireside; and when he thought that such another creature, quite as graceful and as full of promise, might have called him father, and been a spring-time in the haggard winter of his life, his sight grew very dim indeed.

'Belle,' said the husband, turning to his wife with a smile, 'I saw an old friend of yours this afternoon.'

'Who was it?'

'Guess!'

'How can I? Tut, don't I know. Mr Scrooge.'

'Mr Scrooge it was. I passed his office window; and as it was not shut up, and he had a candle inside, I could scarcely help seeing him. His partner lies upon the point of death, I hear; and there he sat alone. Quite alone in the world, I do believe.'

'Remove me! I cannot bear it! Leave me! Take me back. Haunt me no longer!'

As he struggled with the Spirit he was conscious of being exhausted, and overcome by an irresistible drowsiness; and, further, of being in his own bedroom; and had barely time to reel to bed, before he sank into a heavy sleep.

The Second of
the Three Spirits

AWAKING in the middle of a prodigiously tough snore, when the Bell struck One, he lay upon his bed, the very core and centre of a blaze of ruddy light, which streamed upon it when the clock proclaimed the hour. He got up softly and shuffled in his slippers to the door.

The moment Scrooge's hand was on the lock, a strange voice called him by his name, and bade him enter. He obeyed.

It was his own room. There was no doubt about that. But it had undergone a surprising transformation. The walls and ceiling were so hung with living green, that it looked a perfect grove, from every part of which, bright gleaming berries glistened. The crisp leaves of holly, mistletoe, and ivy reflected back the light, as if so many little mirrors had been scattered there; and such a mighty blaze went roaring up the chimney, as that dull petrifaction of a hearth had never known in Scrooge's time, or Marley's, or for many a winter season gone. Heaped up upon the floor, to form a kind of throne, were turkeys, geese, game, brawn, great joints of meat, sucking-pigs, long wreaths of sausages, mince-pies, plum-puddings, barrels of oysters, red-hot chestnuts, cherry-cheeked ap-ples, juicy oranges, luscious pears, immense twelfth-cakes, and seething bowls of punch, that made the chamber dim with their delicious steam. In easy state upon this couch, there sat a jolly Giant, glorious to see; who bore a glowing torch, in shape not unlike Plenty's horn, and held it up, high up, to shed its light on Scrooge, as he came peeping round the door.

'Come in! Come in! and know me better, man! I am the Ghost of Christmas Present. Look upon me!'

Scrooge reverently did so. It was clothed in one simple deep green robe, or mantle, bordered with white fur. This garment hung so loosely on the figure, that its capacious breast was bare. Its feet were also bare; and on its head it wore no other covering than a holly wreath set here and there with shining icicles. Its dark brown curls were long and free: free as its genial face, its sparkling eye, its open hand, its cheery voice, its unconstrained demeanour, and its joyful air.

'You have never seen the like of me before!'

'Never.'

'Have never walked forth with **the** younger members of

my family; meaning (for I am very young) my elder
brothers born in these later years?'

'I don't think I have. I am afraid I have not. Have you
had many brothers, Spirit?'

'More than eighteen hundred.'

'A tremendous family to provide for! Spirit, conduct me
where you will. I went forth last night on compulsion, and
I learnt a lesson which is working now. To-night, if you
have aught to teach me, let me profit by it.'

'Touch my robe!'

Scrooge did as he was told, and held it fast.

Holly, mistletoe, red berries, ivy, turkeys, geese, game,
poultry, brawn, meat, pigs, sausages, oysters, pies, pud-
dings, fruit, and punch, all vanished instantly. So did the
room, the fire, the ruddy glow, the hour of night, and they
stood in the city streets on Christmas morning. The
poulterers' shops were still half open, and the fruiterers'
were radiant in their glory. There were great, round, pot-
bellied baskets of chestnuts, shaped like the waistcoats of
jolly old gentlemen, lolling at the doors, and tumbling out
into the street in their apoplectic opulence. There were
ruddy, brown-faced, broad-girthed Spanish Onions, shining in the fatness of their growth like Spanish Friars; and
winking from their shelves in wanton slyness at the girls as
they went by, and glanced demurely at the hung-up mistletoe. There were pears and apples, clustered high in bloom-
ing pyramids; there were bunches of grapes, made, in the

shopkeepers' benevolence, to dangle from conspicuous hooks, that people's mouths might water gratis as they passed; there were piles of filberts, mossy and brown, recalling, in their fragrance, ancient walks among the woods, and pleasant shufflings ankle deep through withered leaves; there were Norfolk Biffins, squab and swarthy, setting off the yellow of the oranges and lemons, and, in the great compactness of their juicy persons, urgently entreating and beseeching to be carried home in paper bags and eaten after dinner.

The Grocers'! oh the Grocers'! nearly closed, with perhaps two shutters down, or one; but through those gaps such glimpses! The customers were all so hurried and so eager, that they tumbled up against each other. When there were angry words between some who had jostled with each other, the Spirit shed a few drops of water on them from his torch, and their good humour was restored directly. For they said, it was a shame to quarrel upon Christmas Day. And so it was! God love it, so it was!

And perhaps it was the pleasure the good Spirit had in showing off this power of his, or else it was his own kind, generous, hearty nature, and his sympathy with all poor men, that led him straight to Scrooge's clerk's; for there he went, and took Scrooge with him, holding to his robe, and on the threshold of the door the Spirit smiled, and stopped to bless Bob Cratchit's dwelling with the sprinklings of his torch. Think of that! Bob had but fifteen 'Bob' a-week himself; he pocketed on Saturdays but fifteen copies of his Christian name; and yet the Ghost of Christmas Present blessed his four-roomed house!

Then up rose Mrs Cratchit, Cratchit's wife, dressed out but poorly in a twice-turned gown, but brave in ribbons, which are cheap and make a goodly show for sixpence; and she laid the cloth, assisted by Belinda Cratchit, second of her daughters, also brave in ribbons; while Master Peter Cratchit plunged a fork into the saucepan of potatoes, and getting the corners of his monstrous shirt-collar (Bob's private property, conferred upon his son and heir in honour of the day) into his mouth, rejoiced to find himself so gallantly attired, and yearned to show his linen in the fashionable Parks. And now two smaller Cratchits, boy and girl, came tearing in, screaming that outside the baker's they had smelt the goose, and known it for their own; and basking in luxurious thoughts of sage-and-onion, these young Cratchits danced about the table, and exalted Master Peter Cratchit to the skies, while he (not proud, although his collars nearly choked him) blew the fire, until the slow potatoes bubbling up, knocked loudly at the saucepan-lid to be let out and peeled.

'Whatever has got your precious father then,' said Mrs Cratchit. 'And your brother, Tiny Tim! And Martha warn't as late last Christmas Day by half-an-hour!'

'Here's Martha, mother!' said a girl, appearing as she spoke.

'Here's Martha, mother!' cried the two young Cratch-its.' 'Hurrah! There's *such* a goose, Martha!'

'Why, bless your heart alive, my dear, how late you are! Well! Never mind so long as you are come. Sit ye down before the fire, my dear, and have a warm, Lord bless ye!'

'No no! There's father coming,' cried the two young Cratchits, who were everywhere at once. 'Hide Martha, hide!'

So Martha hid herself, and in came little Bob, the father, with at least three feet of comforter exclusive of the fringe, hanging down before him; and his threadbare clothes darned up and brushed, to look seasonable; and Tiny Tim upon his shoulder. Alas for Tiny Tim, he bore a little crutch, and had his limbs supported by an iron frame!

'Why, where's our Martha?' cried Bob Cratchit looking round.

'Not coming.'

'Not coming!' said Bob, with a sudden declension in his high spirits; for he had been Tim's blood horse all the way from church, and had come home rampant. 'Not coming upon Christmas Day!'

Martha didn't like to see him disappointed, if it were only in joke; so she came out prematurely from behind the closet door, and ran into his arms, while the two young Cratchits hustled Tiny Tim, and bore him off into the wash-house, that he might hear the pudding singing in the copper.

'And how did little Tim behave?' asked Mrs Cratchit.

'As good as gold, and better. Somehow he gets thoughtful, sitting by himself so much, and thinks the strangest things you ever heard. He told me, coming home, that he hoped the people saw him in the church, because he was a cripple, and it might be pleasant to them to remember upon Christmas Day, who made lame beggars walk and blind men see.'

Bob's voice was tremulous when he told them this, and trembled more when he said that Tiny Tim was growing strong and hearty.

His active little crutch was heard upon the floor, and back came Tiny Tim before another word was spoken, escorted by his brother and sister to his stool beside the fire; and while Bob, turning up his cuffs — as if, poor fellow, they were capable of being made more shabby — compounded some hot mixture in a jug with gin and lemons, and stirred it round and round and put it on the hob to simmer; Master Peter and the two ubiquitous young Cratchits went to fetch the goose, with which they soon returned in high procession.

Mrs Cratchit made the gravy (ready beforehand in a little saucepan) hissing hot; Master Peter mashed the potatoes with incredible vigour; Miss Belinda sweetened up the apple-sauce; Martha dusted the hot plates; Bob took Tiny Tim beside him in a tiny corner at the table; the two young Cratchits set chairs for everybody, not forgetting themselves, and mounting guard upon their posts, crammed spoons into their mouths, lest they should shriek for goose before their turn came to be helped. At last the dishes were set on, and grace was said. It was succeeded by a breathless pause, as Mrs Cratchit, looking slowly all along the carving-knife, prepared to plunge it in the breast; but when she did, and when the long expected gush of stuffing issued forth, one murmur of delight arose all round the board, and even Tiny Tim, excited by the two young Cratchits, beat on the table with the handle of his knife, and feebly cried Hurrah!

There never was such a goose. Bob said he didn't believe there ever was such a goose cooked. Its tenderness and flavour, size and cheapness, were the themes of universal admiration. Eked out by the apple-sauce and mashed potatoes, it was a sufficient dinner for the whole family; indeed, as Mrs Cratchit said with great delight (surveying one small atom of a bone upon the dish), they hadn't ate it all at last! Yet every one had had enough, and the youngest Cratchits in particular, were steeped in sage and onion to the eyebrows! But now, the plates being changed by Miss Belinda, Mrs Cratchit left the room alone — too nervous to bear witnesses — to take the pudding up, and bring it in.

Suppose it should not be done enough! Suppose it should break in turning out! Suppose somebody should have got over the wall of the back-yard, and stolen it, a supposition at which the two young Cratchits became livid!

Hallo! A great deal of steam! The pudding was out of the copper. A smell like a washing-day! That was the cloth. A smell like an eating-house, and a pastry cook's next door to each other, with a laundress's next door to that! That was the pudding. In half a minute Mrs Cratchit entered: flushed, but smiling proudly: with the pudding, like a speckled cannon-ball, so hard and firm, blazing in half of half-a-quartern of ignited brandy, and bedight with Christmas holly stuck into the top.

Oh, a wonderful pudding! Bob Cratchit said, and calmly too, that he regarded it as the greatest success achieved by Mrs Cratchit since their marriage. Mrs Cratchit said that now the weight was off her mind, she would confess she had had her doubts about the quantity of flour. Everybody had something to say about it, but nobody said or thought it was at all a small pudding for a large family. Any Cratchit would have blushed to hint at such a thing.

At last the dinner was all done, the cloth was cleared, the hearth swept, and the fire made up. The compound in the jug being tasted and considered perfect, apples and oranges were put upon the table, and a shovel-full of chestnuts on the fire. Then all the Cratchit family drew round the hearth, in what Bob Cratchit called a circle, meaning half a one; and at Bob Cratchit's elbow stood the family display of glass; two tumblers, and a custard-cup without a handle.

These held the hot stuff from the jug, however, as well as golden goblets would have done; and Bob served it out with beaming looks, while the chestnuts on the fire sputtered and crackled noisily. Then Bob proposed:

'A Merry Christmas to us all, my dears. God bless us!'

Which all the family re-echoed.

'God bless us every one!' said Tiny Tim, the last of all.

'Spirit,' said Scrooge, with an interest he had never felt before, 'tell me if Tiny Tim will live.'

'I see a vacant seat,' replied the Ghost, 'in the poor chimney corner, and a crutch without an owner, carefully preserved. If these shadows remain unaltered by the Future, the child will die.'

'No, no,' said Scrooge. 'Oh no, kind Spirit! say he will be spared.'

'If these shadows remain unaltered by the Future, none other of my race,' returned the Ghost, 'will find him here. What then? If he be like to die, he had better do it, and decrease the surplus population.'

Scrooge hung his head to hear his own words quoted by the Spirit, and was overcome with penitence and grief.

'Man,' said the Ghost, 'if man you be in heart, not adamant, forbear that wicked cant until you have discovered What the surplus is, and Where it is. Will you decide what men shall live, what men shall die? It may be, that in the sight of Heaven, you are more worthless and less fit to live than millions like this poor man's child.'

'Mr Scrooge!' said Bob; 'I'll give you Mr Scrooge, the Founder of the Feast!'

'The Founder of the Feast indeed!' cried Mrs Cratchit, reddening. 'I wish I had him here. I'd give him a piece of my mind to feast upon, and I hope he'd have a good appetite for it.'

'My dear, the children; Christmas Day.'

'It should be Christmas Day, I am sure, on which one drinks the health of such an odious, stingy, hard, unfeeling man as Mr Scrooge. You know he is, Robert! Nobody knows it better than you do, poor fellow!'

'My dear, Christmas Day.'

'I'll drink his health for your sake and the Day's,' said Mrs Cratchit, 'not for his. Long life to him! A merry Christmas and a happy new year! He'll be very merry and very happy, I have no doubt!'

The children drank the toast after her. It was the first of their proceedings which had no heartiness in it. Tiny Tim drank it last of all, but he didn't care twopence for it. Scrooge was the Ogre of the family. The mention of his name cast a dark shadow on the party, which was not dispelled for full five minutes.

After it had passed away, they were ten times merrier than before. They were happy, grateful, pleased with one another, and contented with the time; and when they faded, and looked happier yet in the bright sprinklings of the Spirit's torch at parting, Scrooge had his eye upon them, and especially on Tiny Tim, until the last.

And now, without a word of warning from the Ghost, they stood upon a bleak and desert moor.

'What place is this?' asked Scrooge.

'A place where Miners live, who labour in the bowels of the earth,' returned the Spirit. 'But they know me. See!'

A light shone from the window of a hut, and swiftly they advanced towards it. Passing through the wall of mud and stone, they found a cheerful company assembled round a glowing fire. An old, old man and woman, with their children and their children's children. The old man, in a voice that seldom rose above the howling of the wind upon the barren waste, was singing them a Christmas song.

The Spirit did not tarry here, but bade Scrooge hold his robe, and passing on above the moor, sped to sea. To Scrooge's horror, looking back, he saw the last of the land, a frightful range of rocks, behind them; and his ears were deafened by the thundering of water.

Built upon a dismal reef of sunken rocks, some league or so from shore, on which the waters chafed and dashed, the wild year through, there stood a solitary lighthouse. But even here, two men who watched the light had made a fire, and joining hands over the rough table they wished each other Merry Christmas in their can of grog.

It was a great surprise to Scrooge, while listening to the moaning of the wind, to hear a hearty laugh. It was a much greater surprise to Scrooge to recognise it as his own nephew's, and to find himself in a bright, dry, gleaming room, with the Spirit standing smiling by his side.

It is a fair, even-handed, noble adjustment of things, that while there is infection in disease and sorrow, there is nothing in the world so irresistibly contagious as laughter and good-humour. When Scrooge's nephew laughed in this way, Scrooge's niece, by marriage, laughed as heartily as he. And their assembled friends being not a bit behindhand, roared out, lustily.

'He said that Christmas was a humbug, as I live!' cried Scrooge's nephew. 'He believed it too!'

'More shame for him, Fred!' said Scrooge's niece, indignantly. Bless those women; they never do anything by halves. They are always in earnest.

She was very pretty: exceedingly pretty with the sunniest pair of eyes you ever saw.

'He's a comical old fellow,' said Scrooge's nephew, 'that's the truth; and not so pleasant as he might be.'

'I'm sure he is very rich, Fred,' hinted Scrooge's niece.

'What of that, my dear!' said Scrooge's nephew. 'His wealth is of no use to him. He don't do any good with it.'

'I have no patience with him,' observed Scrooge's niece.

'Oh, I have! I am sorry for him; I couldn't be angry

with him if I tried. Who suffers by his ill whims? Himself, always. Here, he takes it into his head to dislike us, and he won't come and dine with us. What's the consequence? He don't lose much of a dinner.'

'Indeed, I think he loses a very good dinner,' interrupted Scrooge's niece.

'Well! I am very glad to hear it,' said Scrooge's nephew, 'because I haven't any great faith in these young housekeepers. What do *you* say, Topper?'

Topper had clearly got his eye upon one of Scrooge's niece's sisters, for he answered that a bachelor was a wretched outcast, who had no right to express an opinion on the subject. Whereat Scrooge's niece's sister — the plump one with the lace tucker: blushed.

After a while they played at forfeits; for it is good to be children sometimes, and never better than at Christmas, when its mighty Founder was a child himself. Stop! There was first a game at blind-man's buff. Of course there was. And I no more believe Topper was really blind than I believe he had eyes in his boots. The way he went after that plump sister in the lace tucker, was an outrage on the credulity of human nature. Knocking down the fire-irons, tumbling over the chairs, bumping up against the piano, smothering himself among the curtains, wherever she went, there went he. He always knew where the plump sister was. He wouldn't catch anybody else. If you had fallen up against him, as some of them did, and stood there; he would have made a feint of endeavouring to seize you, which would have been an affront to your understanding; and would instantly have sidled off in the direction of the plump sister. She often cried out that it wasn't fair; and it really was not. But when at last, he caught her; when, in spite of all her silken rustlings, and her rapid flutterings past him, he got her into a corner whence there was no escape; then his conduct was the most execrable. For his pretending not to know her; his pretending that it was necessary to touch her head-dress, and, further to assure himself of her identity by pressing a certain ring upon her finger, and a certain chain about her neck; was vile, monstrous! No doubt she told him her opinion of it, when, another blind-man being in office, they were so very confidential together, behind the curtains.

'Here is a new game,' said Scrooge. 'One half hour, Spirit, only one!'

It was a Game called Yes and No, where Scrooge's nephew had to think of something, and the rest must find out what; he only answering to their questions yes or no as the case was. The brisk fire of questioning to which he was exposed, elicited from him that he was thinking of an animal, a live animal, rather a disagreeable animal, a savage animal, an animal that growled and grunted sometimes, and talked sometimes, and lived in London, and walked about the streets, and wasn't made a show of, and wasn't led by anybody, and didn't live in a menagerie, and was never killed in a market, and was not a horse, or an ass, or a cow, or a bull, or a tiger, or a dog, or a pig, or a cat, or a bear. At every fresh question that was put to him, this nephew burst into a fresh roar of laughter; and was so inexpressibly tickled, that he was obliged to get up off the sofa and stamp. At last the plump sister, falling into a similar state, cried out:

'I have found it out! I know what it is, Fred! I know what it is!'

'What is it?' cried Fred.

'It's your Uncle Scro-o-o-o-oge!'

'He has given us plenty of merriment, I am sure,' said Fred. 'A Merry Christmas and a happy New Year to the old man, whatever he is! Uncle Scrooge!'

But the whole scene passed off in the breath of the last word spoken by his nephew; and Scrooge and the Spirit were again upon their travels.

Much they saw, and far they went, and many homes they visited, but always with a happy end. The Spirit stood beside sick beds, and they were cheerful; on foreign lands, and they were close at home; by struggling men, and they were patient in their greater hope; by poverty, and it was rich. When, looking at the Spirit as they stood together in an open place, he noticed that its hair was grey.

'Are spirits' lives so short?' asked Scrooge.

'My life upon this globe, is very brief,' said the Ghost. 'It ends to-night, to-night at midnight.'

As they stood together in an open space, the bell struck *twelve*.

Scrooge looked about him for the Ghost, and saw it not. As the last stroke ceased to vibrate, he remembered the prediction of old Jacob Marley, and lifting up his eyes, beheld a solemn Phantom, draped and hooded, coming, like a mist along the ground, towards him.

The Last of
the Spirits

IT was shrouded in a deep black garment, which concealed its head, its face, its form, and left nothing of it visible, save one outstretched hand.

'I am in the presence of the Ghost of Christmas Yet To Come?'

The Spirit answered not, but pointed onward with its hand.

'Ghost of the Future, I fear you more than any Spectre I have seen. But, as I know your purpose is to do me good, and as I hope to live to be another man from what I was, I am prepared to bear you company, and do it with a thankful heart. Lead on! Lead on! The night is waning fast, and it is precious time to me, I know. Lead on, Spirit!'

They scarcely seemed to enter the city; for the city rather seemed to spring up about them. But there they were, in the heart of it; on Change, amongst the merchants.

The Spirit stopped beside one little knot of business men. Observing that the hand was pointed to them, Scrooge advanced to listen to their talk.

'No,' said a great fat man with a monstrous chin, 'I don't know much about it, either way. I only know he's dead.'

'When did he die?' inquired another.

'Last night, I believe.'

'What has he done with his money?'

'I haven't heard. He hasn't left it to *me*. That's all I know.'

Scrooge was surprised that the Spirit should attach importance to conversations apparently so trivial. They could scarcely have any bearing on the death of Jacob, his old partner, for that was Past, and this Ghost's province was the Future.

He looked about in that very place for his own image; but another man stood in his accustomed corner, and though the clock pointed to his usual time of day for being there, he saw no likeness of himself among the multitudes.

They left the busy scene, and went into an obscure part of the town, to a low-browed, beetling shop, where iron, old rags, bottles, bones, and greasy offal, were bought by a grey-haired rascal of great age, who sat smoking his pipe in all the luxury of calm retirement.

A woman with a heavy bundle slunk into the shop but she had scarcely entered when another woman simi-

larly laden came in too and she was closely followed by a
man in faded black. After a short period of blank astonishment, in which the old man with the pipe had joined
them, they all three burst into a laugh.

'Let the charwoman alone to be the first!' cried she who
had entered first. 'Let the laundress alone to be the second;
and let the undertaker's man alone to be the third. Look
here, old Joe, here's a chance! If we haven't all three met
here without meaning it!'

'You couldn't have met in a better place. Come into
the parlour. Come into the parlour.'

The woman who had already spoken threw her bundle
on the floor and sat down in a flaunting manner on a stool,
crossing her elbows on her knees, and looking with a bold
defiance at the other two.

'What odds then! What odds, Mrs Dilber? Who's the
worse for the loss of a few things like these? Not a dead
man, I suppose.'

'No, indeed,' said Mrs Dilber, laughing.

'If he wanted to keep 'em after he was dead. A wicked
old screw, why wasn't he natural in his lifetime? If he had
been, he'd have had somebody to look after him when he
was struck with Death, instead of lying gasping out his last
there, alone by himself. Open that bundle, old Joe, and
let me know the value of it. Speak out plain. I'm not
afraid to be the first, nor afraid for them to see it.'

Joe went down on his knees for the greater convenience

48

of opening the bundle, and dragged out a large and heavy roll of some dark stuff.

'What do you call this? Bed-curtains!'

'Ah! Bed-curtains!'

'You don't mean to say you took 'em down, rings and all, with him lying there?' said Joe.

'Yes I do,' replied the woman. 'Why not? Don't drop that oil upon the blankets, now.'

'*His* blankets?' asked Joe.

'Whose else's do you think?' replied the woman. 'He isn't likely to take cold without 'em, I dare say.'

'I hope he didn't die of anything catching? Eh?' said old Joe, stopping in his work, and looking up.

'Don't you be afraid of that,' returned the woman. 'I an't so fond of his company that I'd loiter about him for such things, if he did. Ah! You may look through that shirt till your eyes ache; but you won't find a hole in it, nor a threadbare place. It's the best he had, and a fine one too. They'd have wasted it, if it hadn't been for me.'

'What do you call wasting of it?' asked old Joe.

'Putting it on him to be buried in, to be sure,' replied the woman with a laugh. 'Somebody was fool enough to do it, but I took it off again. If calico an't good enough for such a purpose, it isn't good enough for anything. This is the end of it, you see! He frightened every one away from him when he was alive, to profit us when he was dead! Ha, ha, ha!'

49

'Spirit!' said Scrooge, shuddering from head to foot. 'I see, I see. The case of this unhappy man might be my own. My life tends that way, now. Merciful Heaven, what is this!'

He recoiled in terror, for the scene had changed, and now he almost touched a bed: a bare, uncurtained bed: on which, beneath a ragged sheet, there lay a something covered up, which, though it was dumb, announced itself in awful language. A cat was tearing at the door, and there was a sound of gnawing rats beneath the hearth-stone.

'Spirit! this is a fearful place. In leaving it, I shall not leave its lesson, trust me. Let us go!'

Still the Ghost pointed with an unmoved finger to the head.

'I understand you,' Scrooge returned, 'and I would do it, if I could. But I have not the power, Spirit. I have not the power. Let me see some tenderness connected with a death, or that dark chamber, Spirit, which we left just now, will be for ever present to me.'

The Ghost conducted him through several streets familiar to his feet; and as they went along, Scrooge looked here and there to find himself, but nowhere was he to be seen. They entered poor Bob Cratchit's house; the dwelling he had visited before; and found the mother and the children seated round the fire.

Quiet. Very quiet.

The mother laid her work upon the table, and put her hand up to her face.

'The colour hurts my eyes,' she said.

The colour? Ah, poor Tiny Tim!

'They're better now again,' said Cratchit's wife. 'It makes them weak by candle-light; and I wouldn't show weak eyes to your father when he comes home, for the world. It must be near his time.'

'Past it rather,' Peter answered, shutting up his book. But I think he has walked a little slower than he used, these few last evenings, mother.'

They were very quiet again.

'I have known him walk with — I have known him walk with Tiny Tim upon his shoulder, very fast indeed. But he was very light to carry,' she resumed, intent upon her work, 'and his father loved him so, that it was no trouble: no trouble. And there is your father at the door!'

She hurried out to meet him; and little Bob in his comforter — he had need of it, poor fellow — came in.

'You went to-day then, Robert?' said his wife.

'Yes, my dear,' returned Bob. 'I wish you could have gone. It would have done you good to see how green a place it is. But you'll see it often. I promised him that I would walk there on a Sunday. My little, little child!' cried Bob. 'My little child!'

He broke down all at once. He couldn't help it. If he

could have helped it, he and his child would have been farther apart perhaps than they were.

'Spectre,' said Scrooge, 'something informs me that our parting moment is at hand. I know it, but I know not how. Tell me what man that was whom we saw lying dead?'

The Phantom gave no answer but led him to a churchyard. Here, then, the wretched man whose name he had now to learn, lay underneath the ground. It was a worthy place. Walled in by houses; overrun by grass and weeds.

The Spirit stood among the graves, and pointed down to One.

'Before I draw nearer to that stone to which you point,' said Scrooge, 'answer me one question. Are these the shadows of the things that Will be, or are they shadows of the things that May be, only?'

Still the Ghost pointed downward to the grave by which it stood.

'Men's courses will foreshadow certain ends, to which, if persevered in, they must lead,' said Scrooge. 'But if the courses be departed from, the ends will change. Say it is thus with what you show me!'

The Spirit was immovable as ever.

Scrooge crept towards it, trembling as he went; and following the finger, read upon the stone of the neglected grave his own name, EBENEZER SCROOGE.

'Am *I* that man who lay upon the bed?' he cried, upon his knees.

'No, Spirit! Oh no, no!'

'Spirit!' he cried, tight clutching at its robe, 'hear me!
I am not the man I was. I will not be the man I must have
been but for this intercourse. Why show me this, if I am
past all hope?'

'Good Spirit,' he pursued, as down upon the ground he
fell before it: 'Your nature intercedes for me, and pities me.
Assure me that I yet may change these shadows you have
shown me, by an altered life!'

The kind hand trembled.

'I will honour Christmas in my heart, and try to keep
it all the year. I will live in the Past, the Present, and the
Future. The Spirits of all Three shall strive within me. I
will not shut out the lessons that they teach. Oh, tell me I
may sponge away the writing on this stone!'

In his agony, he caught the spectral hand. It sought to
free itself, but he was strong in his entreaty, and detained
it. The Spirit, stronger yet, repulsed him.

Holding up his hands in one last prayer to have his
fate reversed, he saw an alteration in the Phantom's hood
and dress. It shrank, collapsed, and dwindled down into a
bedpost.

The End of It

YES! and the bedpost was his own. The bed was his own, the room was his own. Best and happiest of all, the time before him was his own, to make amends in!

'I will live in the Past, the Present, and the Future!' Scrooge repeated, as he scrambled out of bed. 'The Spirits of all Three shall strive within me. Oh Jacob Marley! Heaven, and the Christmas Time be praised for this! I say it on my knees, old Jacob; on my knees!'

'They are not torn down,' cried Scrooge, folding one of his bed-curtains in his arms, 'they are not torn down, rings and all. They are here: I am here: the shadows of the things that would have been, may be dispelled. They will be. I know they will!'

His hands were busy with his garments all this time: turning them inside out, putting them on upside down, tearing them, mislaying them.

'I don't know what to do! I am as light as a feather, I am as happy as an angel, I am as merry as a school-boy. I am as giddy as a drunken man. A merry Christmas to everybody! A happy New Year to all the world. Hallo here! Whoop! Hallo!'

He was checked in his transports by the churches ringing out the lustiest peals he had ever heard.

Running to the window, he opened it, and put out his head. No fog, no mist: clear, bright, shining Golden sunlight.

'What's to-day?' cried Scrooge, calling downward to a boy in Sunday clothes, who perhaps had loitered in to look about him.

'Eh?' returned the boy, with all his might of wonder.

'What's to-day, my fine fellow?' said Scrooge.

'To-day!' replied the boy. 'Why, Christmas Day.'

'It's Christmas Day!' said Scrooge to himself. 'I haven't missed it. The Spirits have done it all in one night. They can do anything they like. Of course they can. Of course they can. Hallo, my fine fellow!'

'Hallo!' returned the boy.

'Do you know the Poulterer's, in the next street but one, at the corner?' Scrooge inquired.

'I should hope I did,' replied the lad.

'An intelligent boy!' said Scrooge. 'A remarkable boy! Do you know whether they've sold the prize Turkey that was hanging up there? Not the little prize Turkey; the big one?'

'What, the one as big as me?' returned the boy.

'What a delightful boy!' said Scrooge. 'It's a pleasure to talk to him. Yes, my buck!'

'It's hanging there now,' replied the boy.

'Is it?' said Scrooge. 'Go and buy it.'

'Walk-ER!' exclaimed the boy.

'No, no,' said Scrooge, 'I am in earnest. Go and buy it, and tell 'em to bring it here, that I may give them the direction where to take it. Come back with the man, and I'll give you a shilling. Come back with him in less than five minutes, and I'll give you half-a-crown!'

'I'll send it to Bob Cratchit's!' whispered Scrooge, rubbing his hands, and splitting with a laugh. 'He sha'n't know who sends it. It's twice the size of Tiny Tim.'

It *was* a Turkey! He never could have stood upon his legs, that bird. He would have snapped 'em short off in a minute, like sticks of sealing-wax.

He dressed himself 'all in his best,' and at last got out into the streets.

He had not gone far, when coming on towards him he beheld the portly gentleman, who had walked into his counting-house the day before and said, 'Scrooge and Marley's, I believe?'

'My dear sir,' said Scrooge, quickening his pace, and taking the old gentleman by both his hands. 'How do you do? I hope you succeeded yesterday. It was very kind of you. A merry Christmas to you, sir!'

'Mr Scrooge?'

'Yes,' said Scrooge. 'That is my name, and I fear it may not be pleasant to you. Allow me to ask your pardon. And will you have the goodness —' here Scrooge whispered in his ear.

'Lord bless me!' cried the gentleman, as if his breath were gone. 'My dear Mr Scrooge, are you serious?'

'If you please,' said Scrooge. 'Not a farthing less. A great many back-payments are included in it, I assure you. Will you do me that favour?'

'My dear sir,' said the other, shaking hands with him. 'I don't know what to say to such munifi —'

'Don't say anything, please,' retorted Scrooge. 'Come and see me. Will you come and see me?'

'I will!' cried the old gentleman. And it was clear he meant to do it.

'Thank'ee,' said Scrooge. 'I am much obliged to you. I thank you fifty times. Bless you!'

He went to church, and walked about the streets.

In the afternoon, he turned his steps towards his nephew's house.

He passed the door a dozen times, before he had the courage to go up and knock. But he made a dash, and did it:

'Is your master at home, my dear?' said Scrooge to the girl. Nice girl! Very.

'Yes, sir.'

'Where is he, my love?' said Scrooge.

'He's in the dining-room, sir, along with mistress. I'll show you up stairs, if you please.'

'Thank'ee. He knows me,' said Scrooge, with his hand already on the dining-room lock. 'I'll go in here, my dear.'

'Fred!'

'Why bless my soul!' cried Fred, 'who's that?'

'It's I. Your uncle Scrooge. I have come to dinner. Will you let me in, Fred?'

Let him in! It is a mercy he didn't shake his arm off. He was at home in five minutes. Nothing could be heartier. His niece looked just the same. So did Topper when *he* came. So did the plump sister, when *she* came. So did every one when *they* came. Wonderful party, wonderful games, wonderful unanimity, won-der-ful happiness!

But he was early at the office next morning. Oh he was early there. If he could only be there first, and catch Bob Cratchit coming late! That was the thing he had set his heart upon.

And he did it; yes he did! The clock struck nine. No Bob. A quarter past. No Bob. He was full eighteen minutes and a half, behind his time.

His hat was off, before he opened the door; his comforter too. He was on his stool in a jiffy; driving away with his pen, as if he were trying to overtake nine o'clock.

'Hallo!' growled Scrooge, in his accustomed voice as

near as he could feign it. 'What do you mean by coming here at this time of day?'

'I am very sorry, sir,' said Bob. 'I *am* behind my time.'

'You are?' repeated Scrooge. 'Yes. I think you are. Step this way, if you please.'

'It's only once a year, sir,' pleaded Bob, appearing from the Tank. 'It shall not be repeated. I was making rather merry yesterday, sir.'

'Now, I'll tell you what, my friend,' said Scrooge, 'I am not going to stand this sort of thing any longer. And therefore,' he continued, leaping from his stool, and giving Bob such a dig in the waistcoat that he staggered back into the Tank again: 'and therefore I am about to raise your salary!'

Bob trembled, and got a little nearer to the ruler. He had a momentary idea of knocking Scrooge down with it; holding him; and calling to the people in the court for help and a strait-waistcoat.

'A merry Christmas, Bob!' said Scrooge, with an earnestness that could not be mistaken, as he clapped him on the back. 'A merrier Christmas, Bob, my good fellow, than I have given you, for many a year! I'll raise your salary, and endeavour to assist your struggling family, and we will discuss your affairs this very afternoon, over a Christmas bowl of smoking bishop, Bob! Make up the fires, and buy another coal-scuttle before you dot another i, Bob Cratchit!'

Scrooge was better than his word. He did it all, and infinitely more; and to Tiny Tim, who did NOT die, he was a second father. He became as good a friend, as good a master, and as good a man, as the good old city knew, or any other good old city, town, or borough, in the good old world. Some people laughed to see the alteration in him, but he let them laugh, and little heeded them. His own heart laughed: and that was quite enough for him.

He had no further intercourse with Spirits, but lived in that respect upon the Total Abstinence Principle, ever afterwards; and it was always said of him, that he knew how to keep Christmas well, if any man alive possessed the knowledge. May that be truly said of us, and all of us! And so, as Tiny Tim observed, God Bless Us, Every One!

Epilogue

By John Greaves
Hon. Secretary of the Dickens Fellowship

CHARLES DICKENS loved the theatre all his life. When, at the end of 1852 he completed his tour as an amateur actor, in aid of various charities, his love of the theatre was as great as ever. Remembering his success in reading his books aloud to his friends, as he wrote them, he decided to put his ability in this respect to good purpose by reading for the benefit of Working Men's Institutions. This would enable him still to experience the plaudits of a live audience, which he undoubtedly enjoyed.

From this resolve arose his first reading in public, on 27 December 1853, at the Birmingham Town Hall, in aid of the funds of the Mechanics Institute, and the subject chosen by him was the story written ten years before, 'A Christmas Carol'. Three readings were given altogether, for two of which the Carol was chosen, and his total audience for the three nights was nearly 6,000 people.

In all, he gave 26 readings for charity, 19 of which had 'A Christmas Carol' on the programme. On the first occasion Dickens gave a reading of the Carol lasting three hours, so he must obviously have read practically the whole story. Realising that this was not practicable, either for the reader or for the audience, he contracted the story to a reading lasting two hours. On the next 16 occasions, the Carol was the only item on the programme.

In 1858, Dickens decided to give readings for his own benefit, but from then until 1865 continued to fulfil certain promises to give readings for charitable purposes. For his professional readings he cut the version of the Carol down still further, to last about one hour, and included in the same programme, the Pickwick Trial.

On the last two occasions on which he gave the Carol for charity, Dickens included the Pickwick Trial — at the Paris Embassy, on 30 January 1863, and in the Chatham Lecture Hall, on 19 December 1865, and obviously the shorter cut version was used.

For his Farewell professional reading Dickens again chose 'A Christmas Carol' and the Pickwick Trial for the programme. This was given at St James's Hall, Piccadilly London, and was given before the largest audience that had ever assembled in this hall. George Dolby, his manager, in his book 'Charles Dickens as I knew him', says . . . 'he never read the Carol more earnestly, more fervently, or more effectively than on this occasion. The audience, needless to say, were in supreme sympathy with the reader. Not a word was lost. . . .'

His last words that evening were 'In two short weeks from this time I hope that you may enter in your own homes on a new series of readings at which my assistance will be indispensable, but from these garish lights I vanish now for ever more, with a heartfelt, grateful, respectful, and affectionate farewell.'

And so this wonderful little story that identified Dickens with

Christmas and gave him such joy and sorrow in writing was undoubtedly his favourite and most popular subject for reading
aloud. As he, in writing it had laughed and cried, so his audiences
laughed and cried as he read it to them.